# the GIRL with 500 middle NAMES

# MARGARET PETERSON HADDIX

# the GIRL with 500 middle NAMES

illustrated by Janet Hamlin

SCHOLASTIC INC.

New York  Toronto  London  Auckland  Sydney
Mexico City  New Delhi  Hong Kong  Buenos Aires

With thanks to Ellen Krieger, Gina Thackara,
and the Yarn Shop for their knitting advice

ISBN 0-439-81316-6

12 11 10 9 8                                               10/0

Printed in the U.S.A.                          40

First Scholastic printing, October 2005

Designed by Alexandra Maldonado

The text of this book was set in Hadriano Light.

For Ollie Mae Haddix

# Chapter One

"Good-bye, broken chalkboard," I whispered. "Good-bye, cracked floor."

Cross-eyed Krissy turned around and glared at me. Nobody's supposed to call her that, but everybody does—just not to her face. Krissy had to go through first grade two times, so she's older and bigger than the rest of us third graders. Nobody messes with her. But it's hard not to stare at her eyes. They don't look in the same direction at the same time. At the beginning of last year, I asked her if she could teach me how to do that with my eyes. I thought it was a talent, like whistling or walking on your hands. Cross-eyed Krissy looked at me—first with one eye, then the other—and then she spit right on my shoes. Everybody told me I was

lucky she didn't beat me up.

Now I shrank down in my seat, like I did every time Cross-eyed Krissy turned around.

"What are *you* talking about?" she growled.

I reminded myself I wouldn't see Krissy ever again after today either. I spoke up, bold as brass.

"I'm saying good-bye," I said. "I'm going to a new school on Monday."

"Yeah?" Krissy said.

"Yeah," I said, suddenly too full of my news to keep it to myself. "And it's *nice*. It doesn't have any broken windows at all. It's got carpet three inches thick in all the classrooms, my momma says. And all the kids get to work on computers. And they have a reading corner in the library with fairy-tale people painted on the wall."

Krissy squinted at me. One eye seemed to look off to where one of our classroom windows had been covered with plywood all year long. The other eye just showed white. It was a scary thing, Krissy squinting.

"You're lying," she said, playing with the

bottom part of her desk, where it came loose all the time. It made a tapping noise, like a drum. "There ain't no schools like that."

"Children," our teacher, Mrs. Stockrun, said from behind her desk at the front. "I should not be hearing any noise right now. Aren't you doing your worksheets?"

But she didn't even look up. I think she was reading a magazine. One of the boys blew a spitball at her desk.

"I am *not* lying," I told Krissy.

Cassandra from across the aisle looked over at us.

"She's telling the truth," she told Krissy. "I heard Mrs. Stockrun tell Mrs. Mungo during recess, someone's leaving. 'One less paper to grade,' she said."

I felt sad, all of a sudden, that Mrs. Stockrun wasn't going to miss me any more than that. But I wasn't going to miss her, either.

"So she's leaving," Krissy said, like she didn't want to be proved wrong. "That don't mean she's going someplace nice."

Cassandra was turning a bad word someone had written on the top of her desk into a flower. It had hundreds of petals, and leaves dangling like ivy. It was the prettiest thing I'd ever seen drawn on a desk.

"Oh, she is. I heard that, too," Cassandra said. She heard everything. "Mrs. Stockrun said she's going to the *suburbs*."

Krissy frowned. I wondered if she'd hit Cassandra for talking back to her. I just wanted to get out of this school without seeing another fight. But Krissy was frowning at me.

"How?" she asked. She was puzzled, not mad. "You're just as poor as the rest of us. How you gonna go to a school like that?"

"Sweaters," I said.

# Chapter Two

My mother works magic with yarn.

I've been hearing people say that all my life. Back when I was little, I thought it meant Momma could pull rabbits out of a hat, coins out of an ear. I'd watch her real close, hoping to see a trick. All I ever saw was knitting needles flashing through yarn. Every night I fell asleep to the sound of knitting needles clicking, in rhythm, a lullaby like no other kid's.

Magic.

My momma can make sweaters, scarves, hats, slippers, socks, leg warmers, and anything else anyone might dream up out of yarn. She knits on the bus, going to and from work. She knitted in the hospital that long winter we were waiting for Daddy's

back to heal after he fell, building a sky-scraper. She knits the way other people breathe.

But I never thought knitting had anything to do with school. Then one day last year, Momma picked up a book I'd gotten from the school library.

"What're you learning in school nowadays, honey?" she asked. She started turning pages. Then she snorted as loudly as the horses I'd seen at a petting zoo once. "Oh, come on. Men have too walked on the moon. When was this written?" She flipped the pages more quickly and shook her head. "Can you believe it? This book is older than I am."

That was the beginning.

Momma went and talked to the teacher I had then, Mrs. Raun. Momma was shaking when she came home.

"You cold, Momma?" I asked when she came in the door. It was raining outside, and her shiny black raincoat was wet. Raindrops glistened in her hair, where they'd gotten past her umbrella.

"No, I'm mad," Momma said. But she

pressed her lips together, like she wasn't going to tell me why. She went into the kitchen, where Daddy was drinking coffee. I crept over, close to the wall. I wasn't really eavesdropping, but I could hear just fine.

"That place is a wreck," Momma was complaining. "Broken chalkboards, broken sidewalks, broken windows, broken desks— even the crayons are broken!"

"Last time I checked, kids could draw just as well with broken crayons as whole ones," Daddy drawled.

"And the roof leaks," Momma went on, like she hadn't even heard him. "The whole time I was talking to her teacher, there was this *drip, drip, drip. . . .*"

"Kids can learn in a building with a leaky roof. You just put out a pot or two," Daddy said.

"And the teacher kept saying 'she don't' and 'we done,'" Momma said.

"What's wrong with—oh," Daddy said. "Grammar."

"If the teacher doesn't even talk right, how are the kids going to learn?" Momma asked.

Daddy was silent, but I knew what he was doing. Ever since he hurt his back, he's had to stretch every so often. He moves his back out from the chair and tilts his shoulders back and forth and makes an awful face. Then he pushes his elbows back toward the chair and sighs.

I heard the sigh that meant he was done stretching. Then he said, "Ah, Brenda, not all our teachers were that great, either, back when we were in school. And we didn't exactly go to school in a castle."

"And what kind of an education did we get?" Momma asked.

Daddy didn't answer. After a few minutes, Momma yelled out to me, "Janie, have you done your homework yet?"

For days after that, it was like there was a secret war going on in our house. As soon as I left the room, I'd hear Momma start hissing to Daddy, "Did you see in the paper about the test scores down at Janie's school?" Or, "I hear there were thirty-two serious disciplinary problems this week at Janie's school." Or, "This says the school board wants to fire the principal at Janie's school, but they can't find anyone willing to take his place."

And then the war was over, and Momma was knitting more than ever.

One morning when I was getting ready for school, I picked up a nearly finished sweater Momma had left draped on the couch. It was pink angora and light as a cloud. It was the kind of thing you could picture angels wearing. There were little purple flowers on the front, along with the name SARAH knit right into the sweater.

"Who's Sarah?" I asked.

"Nobody we know. Yet," Momma said, sweeping into the room. "But her mother or grandmother is going to pay one hundred fifty dollars for that sweater at The Specialty Shop."

"Huh?" I said.

"You," Momma said, "are looking at an entrepreneur."

I gave her a blank look.

"I," she announced even more dramatically, "am starting my own business."

She posed, mockingly. She put her hands on her hips and tossed her hair over her shoulder. She raised her chin sassily. She looked kind of silly, since she was still wearing slippers with her dressy work clothes.

Daddy was laughing in the doorway to the kitchen.

"Your momma thinks when I get off disability, her sweaters are going to make it so we can pay to move out somewhere, and you can go to a better school," he said.

Momma stopped posing and shoved the sweater and a couple skeins of yarn into her knitting bag.

"I hope," she said. "That's what I'm praying for."

She gave Daddy and me a kiss each, slipped on her shoes, and rushed out the door.

"Your momma is quite a woman," Daddy said, shaking his head.

For a whole year, Momma knitted sweaters with strange names on the front. Ashley. Leigh. Brittany. Courtney. Laken. Parker. Madison. That store she'd found, The Specialty Shop, loved her. She started getting special orders right away. I'd hear her on the phone.

"They want 'Alexander' *and* a choo-choo train on the front?" Momma would ask. "How big is this kid? Size two?" She'd laugh. "Do they think I'm magic?"

She was. Even Daddy wasn't laughing anymore. In September, right after I started third grade at Clyde Elementary, with Cross-eyed Krissy and Know-it-all Cassandra, I heard Daddy and Momma talking at the kitchen table. Momma was pointing at numbers.

"See, that's the security deposit, and this is the moving expenses, and this is the first month's rent. And after that, if I sell two or three sweaters a month, it'll be enough to cover the extra rent. And we'll still be able to pay on the debt from when you were in the hospital—"

"What if you don't sell two or three sweaters a month?" Daddy asked.

"Then we'll cut a few corners some-where else," Momma said. "But I will. The sweaters are going great! Look how much I made in a year. Don't you see—this is some-thing I'm good at. It's our chance. Janie's chance."

Momma got quiet then. Waiting. Daddy was looking at the numbers.

"You're right," he said slowly. "We can do it."

Momma shrieked and gave him a hug, and then they started kissing. I got out of there, fast.

But that's how I came to be saying good-bye to the broken chalkboard, Cross-eyed Krissy, Mrs. Stockrun, and the rest of Clyde Elementary.

* * *

We moved out over the weekend. Daddy's back was healed enough that he could carry a lot of the furniture himself, if he was careful. Two of his friends from work came out to help.

Momma and I carried boxes. I knew I was supposed to be happy, but I had a jumpy feeling in my stomach. Momma had talked so much about how I was getting out of my horrible school, it was like she kind of forgot to mention we were leaving behind our house, too. I'd never lived anywhere else. I liked our house. I liked how the stairs creaked when you stepped on them just the right way. I liked the porch that wrapped around the front. I liked the trees that dangled branches against my bedroom window.

We were moving into an apartment.

"Brand-new!" Momma had told me a few weeks before. "The drains won't clog. The windows will shut right. The furnace won't break in the middle of winter!"

"But it won't be ours." I pouted.

Momma had laughed.

"Oh, Janie, this house isn't ours, either, you know? We'll just be paying rent to a different person."

*But our house feels like it's ours*, I wanted to say. *It thinks it's ours.* But how could I say that? We were moving because of me.

When everything was out of the house, I walked through the empty rooms, trailing my fingers against the walls. The kitchen looked naked without our old oak table smack in the middle of it. My bedroom looked like a stranger's room without my bed, my dresser, my pictures on the walls.

Momma came and found me and gave me a hug.

"Oh, baby doll, I know it's hard. Be strong, okay? We're doing the right thing."

I watched Daddy's friends drive away all our furniture. Then I got into the front seat of Daddy's pickup truck and waved good-bye to the whole neighborhood. Already it didn't seem like we belonged.

# Chapter Three

Satterthwaite.

That was the name of my new school. When Momma woke me up Monday morning, I lay in bed trying out the name. *Satterthwaite. Satterthwaite. I go to Satterthwaite Elementary School.* I loved it. It rolled off my tongue so elegantly. Not at all like "Clyde." "Clyde Elementary" just stuck in my mouth like a clump of peanut butter.

But it seemed like I should be different, going to a different school.

"Janie, Janie, Janie!" Momma popped her head back in my doorway. "Aren't you up yet? You're going to have to hurry now! Breakfast in five minutes!"

I eased out of bed and stared into the strange closet I still hadn't gotten used to. I pulled out my favorite T-shirt and my favorite jeans. At least they were familiar.

An hour later, Momma was walking me through shiny glass doors that reflected the sun. She turned down a gleaming hallway and pulled me into a huge office, as fancy as the one Momma worked in downtown.

"This is my daughter, Janie Sams," she said, pushing me out in front of her. "She's a new student. I brought her enrollment forms in last week?"

"Ah, yes." The woman behind the counter smiled at me. "Hello, Janie. You'll be in Mrs. Burton's third grade. I'll show you the way."

Momma gave me a hug. I guessed that meant it was time for her to leave. I whispered in her ear, "Momma, I'm scared. I've never been a new student before."

"Sure you have," Momma whispered back. "First day of kindergarten."

"That's not the same. Everyone was new then," I said.

Momma let go. I guess we did look pretty silly, standing there clutching each other and whispering.

"You'll do fine," she said, and gave me that big, confident grin she'd had when she'd joked about being an entrepreneur.

I let the woman from the office walk me down a long, long hall. Clyde Elementary was three stories, and I'd spent my first-grade year in the basement. Satterthwaite was all one level, but it seemed like a couple miles from one end of it to the other.

The carpet was not three inches thick. I think Momma had exaggerated. But it was clean and new, and it cushioned every step I took. Clyde didn't even have carpet, just wood floors gone splintery and concrete floors crumbling under peeling gray paint.

"Here we are!" the woman from the office said brightly.

I followed her through a classroom door.

"Oh, welcome, Janie," a woman said. "I'm Mrs. Burton. We're so glad you'll be joining us!"

Fourteen or fifteen kids stared curiously at me. I stared back. They looked like the kids in department store ads—perfect teeth, perfect hair, perfect clothes.

I remembered that my favorite T-shirt

had a hole, right in the front, where every-one could see. And it was faded. The flower decal on the front was starting to peel off. My favorite jeans were faded too, and the knees were practically worn clear through.

I smiled anyway.

"Hi," I said.

What I wanted to do was go back to Clyde right away and apologize to Cross-eyed Krissy. Was this how she felt when kids stared at her eyes? No wonder she was so mean.

Mrs. Burton was telling me what to do. I made myself listen.

"Janie, you can sit right over there by Kimberly, the girl with the green bow in her hair," she said. "We were just getting ready to start math."

Kimberly kind of waved at me, so I'd know who she was. Besides the green bow, she was wearing a green jumper, a green-flowered shirt, and green-flowered tights. The flowers on the shirt were the same as the flowers on the tights. I'd never seen any-one dressed like that before.

I sat down at a desk that looked so

new, I didn't think anyone had ever sat in it. There wasn't a single word carved or inked or even penciled into the smooth, perfect top.

Kimberly leaned toward me, her bow bobbing in my face.

"That's where my best friend used to sit," she said. "She moved away last month."

"Oh," I said. So the desk had been used before. Did Kimberly mean she didn't like me sitting there?

Kimberly kept staring at me. I didn't think I looked *that* weird. Lots of other kids in the class were wearing jeans and T-shirts. It's just that theirs all looked nicer and newer—like they'd just cut the price tags off that morning. Finally Kimberly gave me a little grin.

"I have sixty-five Beanie Babies," she said.

"Wow," I said.

"How many do you have?" she asked.

I wondered if regular stuffed animals counted. Probably not. I tried to remember if Momma had gotten rid of my Happy

Meal Beanie Babies when we moved.

"None," I said, just in case.

"Really?" Kimberly said, as if she'd never met anyone who didn't have any Beanie Babies before.

I decided to pay attention to math.

Mrs. Burton was talking about subtraction. That made me feel good. Subtraction at Satterthwaite couldn't be any different from subtraction at Clyde.

Yes, it could. Mrs. Burton was writing really, really big numbers on the board.

"Now, can anyone tell me how to subtract one hundred eighty-nine from four hundred sixty-three?" Mrs. Burton said. "Kimberly?"

"Um . . . ," Kimberly said. I figured she was still thinking about Beanie Babies.

I reminded myself there was no one to be scared of at this school. I raised my hand.

"Don't you have to borrow?" I asked.

"I bet that's the name you called it at your other school," Mrs. Burton said with an encouraging smile. "You're right, Janie. I'm glad you know that. But the *new* name for it is 'regrouping.'"

Of course. Everything had to be new at Satterthwaite.

* * *

When I got home from school, Daddy was lying on the couch of our new apartment. He turned off the TV and eased up into a sitting position.

"Sick day?" I asked.

"Uh-huh. Should have let your momma carry the dresser in. But I'll live." He shifted positions. "So how was glorious Satterthwaite?"

"Okay," I said.

"Want a snack?" He shuffled into the kitchen and brought back an apple for each of us. Daddy believes in healthy food.

I took a bite, and the apple made a very satisfying crunch.

"Daddy?" I said, when I'd chewed up that first bite. "How'd Momma pick Satterthwaite as the school for me?"

"It's where her boss's kids go," Daddy said. "She said if it was good enough for Mr. Hodgkins's kids, it *might* be good enough for you." He grinned, real big.

"Oh," I said.

Daddy stopped grinning.

"Why'd you ask?" he said.

"Oh . . . " I chewed for a little while, and decided I could tell Daddy. "I think all the other kids there are a lot richer than me."

"How can you tell?" Daddy asked.

"They have really nice clothes. This one girl, Kimberly, told me she has sixty-five Beanie Babies. And when I was on the bus, I saw some of their houses. They're like mansions!"

Daddy wrinkled his eyebrows together like he always does when he's worried.

"None of those kids teased you about being poor, did they?" he asked.

"No." I shook my head. "Everybody was nice."

"Good," Daddy said. He relaxed his eyebrows. "Just remember, Janie-O, money's not everything. Lots of other things matter more."

I was kind of hoping he'd tell me what those other things were, but he didn't.

# Chapter Four

The next day, Kimberly was dressed all in pink. She even had pink sneakers. I wore my purple jeans and a purple top, but you could tell they hadn't come together.

I decided I should try to make friends with someone else. At the first recess, I asked a girl named Danielle if she wanted to play tetherball with me.

"Sorry," she said. "I'm going to do skip-it with Breanna."

At the lunch recess, I asked Marina if she wanted to jump rope with me.

"Yuka and me are going to swing," she said. "I guess you could come too."

But only two swings were open.

By the third recess, I had it figured out: Danielle and Breanna were best friends.

Marina and Yuka were best friends. Courtney and Nicole were best friends.

In Mrs. Burton's class, that just left Kimberly. And why would she want to be friends with me?

I went to the monkey bars by myself. That's where I was when a boy from my class came over to me.

"You're Janie, right?" he said. "Guess what? Your mom works for my dad. She's his secretary."

I squinted up at him. The sun was in my eyes.

"Is your dad Mr. Hodgkins?" I asked.

"Yep," he said. "He says your mom's a good little worker."

"Good little worker." Those were all nice words, but somehow they sounded bad coming out of his mouth. Back at Clyde, when kids said something bad, they used bad words. Something made me want to hit this kid just for calling my momma "little." She wasn't little. She was—she was an entrepreneur.

Nobody hit anybody at Satterthwaite.

"My momma works hard," I said instead.

"Really hard." And I glared, to make this kid understand that that didn't make her a "good little worker."

He backed away.

"Yeah," he mumbled. "Bye!"

As soon as he was gone, I climbed up and did a backward flip on the top bar of the monkey bars. I never would have dared try anything like that back at Clyde.

"Wow!" said a girl below me. It was Kimberly. "How did you do that?"

I looked at Kimberly in her perfect, all-pink outfit.

"First," I said, "you have to be really, really brave."

I was glad that the end-of-recess bell rang just then and I didn't have to say anything else.

# Chapter Five

I may not have had the right clothes, and it was taking longer than I thought to make friends. But I was caught up in math within a week. Mrs. Burton moved me out of the lowest reading group after the first day. And I didn't forget my homework once, even though lots of other kids did.

"I had soccer practice last night," Josh Hodgkins whined when Mrs. Burton asked him why his wasn't finished. "I didn't have time."

Mrs. Burton frowned, which was about the meanest thing she ever did.

"School should come first," she said. "I'll have to write a note to your parents." She looked around the class. "Janie, would you show Josh how to do problem number five in the book?"

I went over to his desk. I decided I shouldn't ask him why he wasn't a "good little worker."

"She gives too much homework," Josh griped.

I shrugged. Josh kept complaining.

"Who cares about fractions, anyway?"

"I think grown-ups have to know them," I said. I didn't mind fractions. I thought they were kind of like a game. But did they give you some test when you became an adult, that had "one-eighth plus one-half" on it?

"When I'm a grown-up," Josh said, "if I need to do any math, I'll hire someone else to do it for me." He looked straight at me. "What's it to you? You probably like homework. 'Cause you can't afford to join a soccer team or anything like that."

For a whole minute, I felt like I couldn't breathe. I felt like Josh had socked me in the stomach. A kid at my old school did that to me once, when I didn't get out of his way when he wanted me to.

Mrs. Burton picked that moment to come over and check on Josh and me.

"Are you two doing all right?" she asked, leaning over so close I could smell her perfume. Her expensive perfume.

"Fine," Josh said.

"Great," I said.

\* \* \*

It got cold.

Now when we went out at recess, our breath made little clouds around our mouths. The bars of the jungle gym felt icy through my gloves.

I guess even Satterthwaite School couldn't afford to heat the playground.

I wouldn't have minded, except that my wrists stuck out of all my winter clothes from last year. The sweatshirts barely came down to my belly button. My winter coat—the same one I'd had since first grade—was even worse. Momma gasped the first morning I tugged it on.

"Well, *that* doesn't fit anymore, does it?" she said.

I shook my head.

"We'll have to put a brick on her head,"

Dad said from the kitchen. "Keep her from growing."

"Not my big girl," Momma said. She hugged my shoulders, as if to protect me from any bricks. "We're proud you're growing, honey. I just didn't expect winter to come on so soon." She peered into the closet, as if hoping some nice, warm—*big*—coat would appear in there by magic. She sighed. "I'll pick up my check at The Specialty Shop this weekend, and then we'll go shopping. I'm sorry, Janie. You'll just have to make do with this coat until then."

I sat on the school bus wondering what Josh Hodgkins would have to say about a ragged, limp, pink coat with a broken zipper. This coat belonged back at Clyde, where everything was broken.

But Josh didn't say anything. Kimberly did.

The second day I wore that coat, she sidled up to me on the playground. *Her* coat was royal blue with red trim. I think I saw a picture once of a princess wearing a coat like that.

"Janie?" she said in a near-whisper. "I have an old coat at home, and my mom says

I can give it to you, if I want. I mean, it's not that old, it's just that I got too big for it. And *you* wouldn't be too big for it, 'cause I'm kind of fat, and you're not."

My face felt too hot and too cold, all at once. I think my tongue was frozen, but my cheeks were on fire. Kimberly was looking at me, waiting. Her face was all scrunched up, like she was really worried about what I might say.

"So do you want it?" Kimberly asked.

"No," I said, because I didn't. I didn't want anyone's hand-me-downs. Then I tried to think what Momma would want me to say. "No, thank you. I'm going to get a new coat on Saturday. My momma and I just haven't had time to shop. That's why I'm wearing this." I shrugged my shoulders, moving my horrible old coat up and down. A little piece of gray stuffing fell out from the coat. Both Kimberly and I watched that stuffing drop to the ground. Then we both looked away, like something really embarrassing had happened. Like one of us had peed her pants or something.

"Oh," Kimberly said. She had the same

look on her face she got when Mrs. Burton asked her about multiplication. Like her brain would never in a million years tell her what to say next.

"Want to go teeter-totter?" I asked her.

"Yes!" she said.

That afternoon, Mrs. Burton made us do three pages in our math journals. She made us look up ten science terms. She made us write sentences for all twenty of our spelling words. I worked *hard*.

But I could still hear Kimberly's voice, echoing in my ears, "So do you want it?" I could still see Kimberly's face in my mind's eye, looking at me like I was really, really poor.

I felt like Saturday would never come.

# Chapter Six

Saturday did come, after all.

I woke up early and lay in bed imagining all the beautiful clothes Momma and I would buy that day. By tonight, I'd have dozens of outfits, just as pretty and rich-looking and matched as Kimberly's. I'd have a warm coat that a princess—no, a queen!—would be proud to call her own. I'd have shoes that hadn't come from Payless, with a label on the side that everybody knew. By the end of the day, I'd look like I belonged at Satterthwaite.

I smelled the coffee that meant Momma and Daddy were up and in the kitchen, reading the newspaper. I slipped out of bed, pulled on my clothes, and sprinted to the door.

"Ready to go, Momma?" I asked.

Momma was still wearing her robe. Her hair stuck out all over her head. She laughed.

"And good morning to you, too, eager beaver," she said. "Don't you know The Specialty Shop doesn't open until ten?"

Three *long* hours later, Momma and I were sitting in our truck, heading to The Specialty Shop. Momma was humming along with the radio.

"This is going to be fun, isn't it?" she asked as she pulled out of our parking lot. "Just us girls, shopping."

That made me feel older, somehow, like Momma and I were the same age, two friends going shopping together. I sat up straighter.

The Specialty Shop was even farther out of the city than Satterthwaite School. It was on a quiet street with lots of trees and lots of other ritzy-looking shops: a jeweler's, a bakery called Crème de la Crème, something called The Stanhope House.

"They say this is what shops in Europe look like," Momma said. "Maybe you'll get to go there someday."

She parked the truck, and we got out. Leaves crunched under our feet. Momma held open The Specialty Shop's heavy wood door for me.

"If you want, you can look around while I talk to the manager," Momma said. "I shouldn't be long."

But something about The Specialty Shop made me want to stick close to Momma. It was the kind of place that made you feel like it might cost money to breathe in there.

We walked up to the fancy, old-fashioned cash register. Then I saw a skinny computer next to it. That was probably what they really used.

"Is Mr. Creston in?" Momma asked the woman behind the counter. She was tall and thin, and wore her hair pulled back like a ballerina's.

"Whom shall I say is calling?" the woman asked haughtily.

"Brenda Sams," Momma said. She had her jaw set, just like she did when she and Daddy were having a fight. As soon as the woman walked away from the cash register, Momma bent down and whispered to me,

"She *knows* who I am. And that's not even talking right. What do you bet she just likes to say 'whom'?"

The woman came back and said, "He can see you now."

Momma turned around and rolled her eyes at me. It was hard not to giggle.

I followed Momma past racks of clothes like Kimberly wore. I saw a price tag: one hundred dollars for a skirt. A plain, black skirt! Okay, so maybe Momma and I wouldn't be buying clothes like Kimberly's. But they'd still be nice. They'd still make me fit in at Satterthwaite.

Momma led me to a fancy carved door at the back of the store. She knocked lightly.

"Mr. Creston?" she called as she turned the knob.

He was on the phone. He held up his hand, like it was sign language for, *Just a minute, just a minute, I'll be right with you.*

Mr. Creston was wearing a suit, which I thought was pretty funny for a Saturday. But he was the kind of person you couldn't have pictured without a suit and tie. Even his hair looked rich. It was dark brown and glossy, like he polished it.

"Great! I'll buy those shares," he was saying into the phone. "Thanks for the tip." He hung up.

As soon as he turned to Momma, he put on a different expression, like a mask. It made me think of the doctors coming into Daddy's hospital room when he was hurt. Mr. Creston looked like those doctors did right before they said, "I'm so sorry. The X rays don't look good. . . ."

"I'm so sorry, Mrs. Sams," Mr. Creston was saying. (How had I known?) "I've been meaning to call you to come pick up your merchandise."

"What?" Momma said. "I came for my check."

"Well—" Mr. Creston looked at Momma and then at me. Then he looked back at Momma. "That's what I needed to talk to you about. It appears that name sweaters are a bit passé now. We're just not getting enough orders. I'm sorry. That's why I'm returning all your samples." He pointed to two bags leaning against the wall behind us. Garbage bags.

I didn't know what "passé" meant, but I could tell it wasn't good.

Momma whirled around and grabbed the nearest bag. She ripped it open. I could see sweater after sweater after sweater. Sweaters I'd been watching Momma knit for months.

"But these aren't just my samples. Some of these were special orders!" Momma protested.

"Yes, but—" Mr. Creston shrugged. "People change their minds. And, you know, Mrs. Sams. The customer is always right."

Momma looked at me. I thought about the beautiful new coat we were going to buy. I thought about the new matching outfit I wanted to wear to school Monday morning. Momma must have been thinking about those things too.

"Don't I have any money coming?" she asked. "Haven't you sold any of my sweaters since the last time?"

Mr. Creston shook his head.

Momma turned, as if she was going to pick up the bags and walk out. They'd be heavy. There were a lot of sweaters in those bags.

Then Momma saw me watching her. She turned back around. Her face was pale, but she had two angry red spots high on her cheekbones.

"Janie, would you please go wait for me in the truck?" she said quietly.

I nodded. I knew better than to mess with Momma when she had that look on her face.

Momma handed me the keys to the truck. I all but tiptoed out. Without Momma, I wasn't sure I'd even be able to open The Specialty Shop's door. I had to push really hard.

And then I sat for what felt like hours, waiting for Momma to come out. I stared at The Specialty Shop's front window, which showed all sorts of sweaters with all sorts of designs. One sweater had sheep jumping over a fence. Another sweater had berries and apples. Another sweater showed flowers growing on a picket fence. I thought probably Momma was telling Mr. Creston that name sweaters weren't the only thing

she could knit. If name sweaters were passé—whatever that meant—it looked like sheep sweaters and apple sweaters and flower sweaters weren't. Probably Momma had convinced Mr. Creston to give her a check ahead of time, because the new kind of sweaters she was going to knit for him would be so great.

But when Momma finally came out, I knew that wasn't true. She was doing her angry walk. Her face was paler than ever. She heaved the bags of sweaters into the back of the truck. Then she slid onto the seat beside me and silently took the keys I held out to her.

She started the truck and backed out.

"Well, let's go shopping," she said. "We won't let *that* ruin our day."

But her voice shook. Her eyes glittered, like they were wetter than they were supposed to be.

"Mr. Creston didn't give you a check, did he?" I asked in a small voice. "He's not going to buy any more of your sweaters, is he?"

"No," Momma said. Her voice was steadier now. "But I got him to tell me the truth. He found someone who can get women in Mexico to knit sweaters really cheap. So he makes more money if he sells those sweaters instead of mine. Even for some of the special orders I already made. . . . And I was too stupid to get him to sign a contract, so he can do that, hand back months of my hard work, just like that . . ." Her voice was rising. She broke off.

"Why don't you just let him pay you what he's going to pay the Mexican women?" I asked.

"Those starvation wages? My time's worth more than that," she snapped. "So's theirs, I think, but"—she glanced over at me—"oh, Janie, this is all grown-up stuff. Don't worry about it. We can still get your clothes today. We'll be fine."

But she didn't sound fine. I didn't feel fine.

# Chapter Seven

Momma didn't say anything for a long time after that. I stared out the window at the cars and trucks and SUVs driving around us. Most of them were nicer than our truck—newer, bigger, shinier. I thought about what Daddy had said, about money not being everything, and it seemed like he'd been lying. Money was the difference between Satterthwaite and Clyde schools. Money was the difference between Kimberly's nice clothes and my old, worn-out ones. Money was the difference between Josh Hodgkins getting to play soccer and me having nothing but school.

Momma turned in at Wal-Mart.

"Here we are!" she said in a faky, bright voice. "What'll it be first? Girls' coats?"

48

We found a rack of pink and purple and blue and orange coats. They mostly looked plastic. Princesses did not wear these coats.

"Which one do you like best?" Momma asked, still trying to sound cheerful. "You can choose whatever you want."

But I saw her turning over the price tags, glancing quickly when she thought I wasn't looking. I watched her fingers flashing through the coats as gracefully as they flashed through yarn.

Through yarn. Suddenly I couldn't even see the coats. All I could see was Momma's hands. I remembered how she'd knitted and knitted and knitted, early in the morning and late at night, on the bus and at home, every second she could for a solid year. Just for me. Because she loved me.

I thought maybe Daddy was right, after all, and some things did matter more than money.

And then I knew what I had to do.

"Momma," I started. I cleared my throat. "Momma, I don't need any new clothes."

Momma stopped in the middle of feeling a purple coat's lining.

"What?" she said. "Of course you do." She looked at me carefully. "This is because of Mr. Creston, isn't it? Really, honey, you don't have to worry about that. It's not your problem. Let's forget that nasty man and just enjoy picking out everything you need."

Her voice was wobbly. Like my knees.

"No," I made myself say. Then my legs were steady again. This was important. I took one last look at the brightly colored coats in front of me and backed away.

"Janie, what are you talking about?" Momma said. "You wear that old coat of yours one more day, it's liable to fall apart. And you don't have a single long-sleeved top that isn't a complete disgrace. I feel like a negligent mother already, letting you go this long without new winter clothes."

I told Momma my plan. I wasn't sure what to be more scared of: that she wouldn't agree, or that she would.

She agreed.

And that's when I knew how bad off we really were.

* * *

I thought calling Kimberly would be the hardest thing in the world.

"Do-you-still-have-that-old-coat-you-said-I-could-have?" I said, as fast as I could, to get it over with. But then I had to say it all over again, because Kimberly hadn't understood a single word.

And then, I couldn't just go get the coat. Kimberly had to talk to her mom, and her mom had to talk to Momma. I heard Momma say, "We had a financial setback recently—no, no, we're fine otherwise. That's very kind of you, but it isn't necessary. . . ." The whole time she looked sick to her stomach. And then it was decided that I would go over to Kimberly's house and play for a while, when I got the coat.

Kimberly's house was big.

She had a playroom the size of our entire apartment.

I didn't have any fun.

The coat itself was red, and looked just as new as anything at Wal-Mart. I wondered if Kimberly had worn it more than once.

I hoped not. I hoped that no one at

Satterthwaite but me and Kimberly would know that my new coat used to belong to her.

I knew somebody would. Probably everybody would.

So getting the coat was hard.

But it was even harder, Monday morning, when I got up and put on a sweater with someone else's name on it.

I picked out the prettiest one of all. It was a soft, snowy white, with ivy leaves on the front and back, and winding along the cuffs. But right smack dab in the front, where everyone was bound to see, the sweater said, ALEXANDRIA.

I didn't glance in the mirror after I pulled the sweater over my head. I put on my old jeans with it. Then I went straight out to breakfast.

Momma looked hard at me when I sat down at the table.

"Oh, Janie, you don't have to do this," she said. "We can buy you *some* new clothes. I'm going to be working a lot of overtime this week to make up for—you know. But as soon as I can, I'll take the names off some of those sweaters, maybe

put your name on instead. So everyone knows it's yours."

I didn't say anything. Momma mumbled, "I should have done that yesterday. But I just couldn't."

I wasn't sure she meant for me to hear that last part. But I remembered the night before. I'd walked into the living room and found Momma sitting on the couch, holding one of the sweaters. She wasn't ripping out stitches. She wasn't knitting. She was just staring at the sweater and crying.

Remembering that, I knew I was doing the right thing.

"This is what I want to wear today," I said now. "Please?"

I was afraid Momma was going to cry again. I didn't want to see that. I looked straight into my cereal bowl.

"Janie—," Daddy said, but didn't go on.

I poured the milk on my cereal. I brought spoonfuls of Cheerios up to my mouth. I drank my orange juice. I didn't look up, but I could feel Momma and Daddy having a conversation over my head, without saying a single word. It was like their eyes were sending secret messages, back and forth. And my ears could hear what they weren't saying. *We can't let her do this. . . . But she says she wants to. . . . This is our fault. . . . But what can we do?*

Finally, Daddy said, "Janie? That sweater looks beautiful on you."

And Momma said, "But you look beautiful in everything you wear. Don't let anyone tell you different."

I finished my breakfast and hugged my parents and put on Kimberly's old red coat. And then I went outside to wait for the bus.

# Chapter Eight

"That's not your name," the girl beside me said as I was hanging up my coat. She was reading my sweater.

I made sure Kimberly's old coat was balanced exactly on the hook. Then I turned around.

I was going to explain. But it was such a *long* story. *My mother made this sweater for me—not to wear, that is; she knows what my name is, of course—but so she could sell it and we could move and I could go to school here instead of at Clyde, where everything's broken and the teachers don't care and the kids beat you up if you don't watch out. But then Mr. Creston was mean, and he said he couldn't sell this, and so he returned it,* and I knew we didn't have lots of extra money to buy me new clothes, and then I decided Momma's sweaters would be my new clothes. Because she loves me. Because—

Okay, it was a *really* long story. And it probably wouldn't make sense to anybody but me. It didn't even make sense to Momma and Daddy.

The girl, Courtney, was still waiting for an answer.

"Maybe Alexandria is my middle name," I said.

"Janie Alexandria Sams?" the girl said. "That's pretty. I wish *my* middle name was Alexandria."

She smiled at me. I smiled at her. I sat down feeling better than I'd felt since Saturday.

In the middle of handing back our spelling tests, Mrs. Burton stopped by my desk.

"That's a beautiful sweater," she said. "I love the ivy. What does it say?" I straightened up so she could see. "Alexandria?" she asked, puzzled.

"It's her middle name," Kimberly volunteered from the next seat over.

Had she been listening to what I'd told Courtney? I gave Kimberly a nasty look, then turned my head back to Mrs. Burton.

"Ah," Mrs. Burton said. She still looked a little puzzled. "Did someone knit that for you?"

"My momma," I said proudly.

"I wish I could knit like that," Mrs. Burton said. "No—I wish my mother could. It must be wonderful having somebody who can knit sweaters like that for you."

She put my spelling test on my desk. I got a 100 and a GREAT JOB! sticker. Some of the butterflies in my stomach stopped flying around. Mrs. Burton leaned over and whispered in my ear: "But my middle name is Gertrude, so I'd never want to advertise that!"

She gave me a little wink, like we shared a secret now.

Poor Mrs. Burton. Gertrude?

By the end of the day, I'd said "It's my middle name" about fifty times. Nobody had recognized Kimberly's old coat, and

I'd mostly managed to avoid her so *she* wouldn't say anything about it. I was feeling pretty good.

But it was only Monday.

# Chapter Nine

On Tuesday, I picked out a beautiful purple sweater with a rainbow across the front. And on each color of the rainbow was a different letter: L-I-N-D-S-A-Y. Lindsay.

I was feeling a little bad about lying about my middle name all day Monday. Today, I decided, I'd tell the truth. I'd have to.

But Josh was the first person who asked.

"What'd you do, *Janie?*" he jeered as I moved the marker on Mrs. Burton's chart to show that I'd packed my lunch instead of buying. "Steal that sweater?"

"No," I said, trying to sound calm. But I could feel all the blood rushing to my face. I could tell that everyone was listening.

"We know Lindsay isn't your first name. And you said yesterday that your middle name is Alexandria. So—"

"Some people have more than one middle name," I said.

"Yeah? How many do you have?" he asked.

"I'm not sure you can count that high," I said.

Well, it was true. The way Josh acted, I wasn't sure he could count at all.

"He made it to four hundred and ninety-nine at the speed-counting contest last year," Kimberly said helpfully. I hadn't even seen her walk over behind me. I looked from Kimberly to Josh.

"Then I must have five hundred middle names, huh?" I said. "At least."

I saw Mrs. Burton watching us with a funny look on her face.

"Time to settle down, class," she said. Unlike Mrs. Stockrun, she sounded like she really meant it. "Now. Take your seats."

We did math and social studies and science. Then, when it was time for our first recess, Mrs. Burton pulled me out of the line.

"I wanted to talk to you for just a minute, Janie," she said.

We waited until everyone else had stampeded outside.

"Is there anything you'd like to tell me?" Mrs. Burton asked. "You aren't having problems at home, are you? Anything wrong at all?"

I shook my head.

"Nope. I mean, no, ma'am."

Mrs. Burton got squinchy lines around her eyes, like she was thinking hard. Her glance flickered down to the big, bold LINDSAY on my sweater, then came back up to my face.

"Are you feeling comfortable at Satterthwaite?" she asked. "I know, when you're new someplace, it takes a while to feel like you fit in."

I wondered just how smart Mrs. Burton was supposed to be. Did I look like I fit in? Actually, with this sweater on, maybe I kind of did. As long as you didn't look at my jeans or my old shoes.

"I like Satterthwaite," I said.

Mrs. Burton relaxed a little bit.

"Well, you're certainly doing very well," she said. She gave me one of those broad smiles that all the teachers at Satterthwaite used. "When I saw which school you were transferring from, I was a little concerned that you might not be, um, prepared. But I'm always delighted to have such a hard worker in my class. I believe you've even spurred on some of the other children who aren't normally as motivated."

I had?

"Keep up the good work," Mrs. Burton said. "And that is certainly another lovely sweater. Did your mother knit this one too?"

"Yes," I said. "She sells them."

"Oh," Mrs. Burton said. "Does she have a catalog? I might be interested in looking at that sometime."

"I'll tell her that," I said, and raced out to the playground with ideas tumbling through my mind. I was so excited all of a sudden, I forgot to worry that someone might recognize Kimberly's old coat.

# Chapter Ten

"No," Momma said.

We were eating dinner, and I had just spilled out everything. Okay, not everything. The important parts. How everyone had been admiring my sweaters the past two days. How Mrs. Burton wanted to see a catalog, if Momma had one. How maybe Mrs. Burton would buy some of Momma's sweaters, and maybe other people would too. How maybe Momma could even have a store of her own, better than Mr. Creston's. That would show him. That would show everyone.

"Oh, Janie," Momma said, shaking her head. "Is *that* why you've insisted on wearing those sweaters? Because you thought people would want to buy them? I'm glad

you wanted to help, but—" She looked at Daddy like she thought he could explain. He was watching her.

None of us was paying attention to the tuna noodle casserole on our plates.

"Janie, it's like this," Momma said. "I lost a lot of money, paying for all the yarn for those sweaters. I can't afford to get burned again. Just printing a catalog would be—well, we don't have that kind of money."

"Well, maybe you wouldn't have to have a catalog," I argued. "Mrs. Burton would understand—"

"No," Momma said again, and her voice was like iron. "It's not worth it. I have to stick to the work I know I'll get paid for."

I must have looked scared, because Mom's expression softened then. She gave me a little smile. "Anyhow, I don't like the idea of using you like—like a billboard or something. A walking ad. You're going to school to learn, not to sell sweaters."

Daddy nodded. I could tell he liked what Momma said.

I didn't.

"But, Momma," I said. "I can learn *and*

sell sweaters. It's not hurting me to do two things at once."

Momma laughed.

"Oh, Janie, I wish I had your faith that everything would work out well. Stay a kid for a while longer, okay? Leave the money worries to Daddy and me." She got up and put her plate in the sink. She brought a pack of oatmeal cookies back to the table. She kissed the top of my head on her way past. "And do me a favor, all right? Wear a sweatshirt tomorrow. Then I'm sure I can finish making over a sweater for you by Thursday. Without a name."

* * *

The next day, I woke up really, really early. The streetlights were still on. I lay in bed and tried to decide what to wear to school.

If I wore another name sweater, Momma would be upset. I didn't want to upset Momma.

But if I wore a sweatshirt, it'd be like giving up. The sweaters were important.

That morning I put on a sweater that was the same blue as the sky on the nicest day of summer. Two birds held up a banner on the front. The banner said, CLAIRE.

Momma looked very disappointed at breakfast. Daddy looked worried.

But neither of them made me go back and change.

The gym teacher called me "Claire" during dodgeball that morning.

"Her name's Janie, remember?" Kimberly told her. "Claire's just one of her middle names."

"You trying to confuse me, kid?" the gym teacher asked.

"No, sir," I said.

The gym teacher shook his head.

Kimberly bent down to pick up a ball. I saw that there were letters on the ribbon hanging from her hair bow. A-L-L-Y . . .

I tapped her on the shoulder.

"Is your middle name Allyson?" I asked.

Kimberly nodded.

"I like that better than Kimberly," she said. "I'm glad you started the middle name trend."

"I did?" I said.

"Do you suppose I can get Mr. Wynans to call me Allyson?"

"Probably," I said. "If you wear your middle name a lot. Since you just have one."

I jumped out of the way of a ball that whizzed toward me. I felt Kimberly's eyes on me. I'd barely spoken to her since she'd given me her coat.

"Do you really have five hundred middle names?" Kimberly asked.

"What do you think?" I asked.

I sounded really rude. Momma would have been ashamed. But it wasn't fair. Kimberly had more clothes than anyone. She had her own playroom. She had so many coats, she could just give them away and never even notice.

I ran away from Kimberly. I grabbed a ball and threw it at the other team as hard as I could.

# Chapter Eleven

On Thursday morning when I woke up there was a beautiful purple sweater hanging on my closet door. It had a pink heart right smack in the middle of the front. And there wasn't a single letter on it spelling out a name—mine or anyone else's.

I held the sweater up to my cheek and felt how soft and warm it was. Then I carefully folded it up and put it in my dresser drawer. I put on another sweater, a green one that proclaimed MELINDA to the whole world.

Momma was there, frowning, as soon as I stepped out of my room.

"Didn't you see the sweater I made over, just for you?" she asked.

"Yes," I said. "Thanks. But lots of kids

are wearing name clothes at my school now. With all sorts of names. I started a trend!"

"Really?" Momma said. She took a step back. "You did?"

"Well, sort of," I said. I didn't think something just Kimberly and I did could really be called a trend. But I felt strangely happy remembering the ALLYSON on Kimberly's ribbon.

Then I noticed the dark circles under Momma's eyes, and I felt guilty. Momma hadn't gotten home from work until after dinner the night before. She must have stayed up really late finishing my other sweater. I knew I should go back and change.

But I didn't.

That morning during science, I got called out of class to go talk to the guidance counselor, Mrs. Wood.

Mrs. Wood was a big woman. Really big. If you saw her from behind, wearing pants, you might think she was a man. Maybe even a football player. But today she was wearing a silky dress with a pink jacket. She had the same kind of smile as Mrs. Burton.

"Now, don't think you're in any trouble, because you're not," she said as soon as I sat down. "I just like to get acquainted with all of Satterthwaite's new students. Now your name is—"

I saw her looking at my sweater.

"Janie Sams," I said.

"Ah," she said, still looking at my sweater. I felt like each letter of MELINDA was as big as Mrs. Wood. I felt like it was written in neon, instead of yarn.

"Just Janie?" Mrs. Wood said. "You don't go by a middle name?"

"No." I shook my head.

"Then why are you wearing that sweater?" Mrs. Wood asked.

I hadn't even been able to explain that very well to my parents. There was no way I was going to try with Mrs. Wood.

"Just because," I said. "I wanted to."

"You don't wish you were someone else, do you?" Mrs. Wood asked.

I thought about that. If I weren't me, who would I be? I thought about the girls who were supposed to get these sweaters—rich kids whose moms or grandmothers maybe hadn't even bothered to pick up what they'd ordered.

If my momma ordered something for me, you know she'd pick it up.

I didn't want to be the real Melinda, Claire, Lindsay, or Alexandria.

I thought about Kimberly. She had everything. Did I want to be her?

Except she didn't understand math, and I did. She got a panicked look on her face every single time Mrs. Burton said, "Now, take out your math books. . . ."

I didn't want to be Kimberly.

"No," I told Mrs. Wood. "I like being me."

Something happened behind Mrs. Wood's smile. She kept smiling, but it didn't look the same anymore. I think she thought I was going to say something else.

"Well," Mrs. Wood said. "That's great!"

When I got back to class, someone had put something on my chair. It was a piece of paper folded over and over, until it was smaller than my thumb. I unfolded it in my lap.

It was from Kimberly.

She had written, *I think you could have 500 middle names if you wanted to.*

I looked over to where Kimberly had her head bent over her science book. *Who asked you?* I wanted to say. Then I remembered: I had. Yesterday during gym I had asked her, "What do you think?"

Kimberly looked up just then, and I stared at her. For once I wasn't just seeing her clothes. She had pale eyes that looked worried. She had a lot of freckles on her cheeks. The corners of her mouth kind of half curled up, like she wanted to smile but was afraid to.

Kimberly wouldn't have lasted a day back at Clyde Elementary. Mean old Krissy would have torn her to shreds. Cassandra would have talked her to death. Kimberly would have cried when the boys were throwing spitballs.

I could really hurt her if I wrote back, *Who asked you?*

I pulled out a fresh sheet of paper.

*I think you could have 500 middle names too. If you wanted*, I wrote carefully. And then I slid the paper across the aisle and watched Kimberly read it.

Kimberly smiled. And, for the first time since she'd given me her coat, I smiled back.

\* \* \*

The phone rang that night while we were eating dinner.

"Let the answering machine get it," Momma said. "This is family time."

But we all listened to the message as it recorded: "Hello, um, this is James Creston from The Specialty Shop. I've run into some shipping problems with the sweaters from Mexico, and I'm getting increased demand for name sweaters. Anyhow, I believe we dissolved our business relation-ship prematurely, and I hoped—"

I didn't hear the rest. I was too busy yelling, "Hooray!"

Momma went over and replayed the message again two times, just to make sure we'd heard it right.

"You'll make him sign a contract this time, right?" I asked anxiously.

Momma was standing there dazed. "I don't know," she said. "Why should he make all the profit from my sweaters?"

"He shouldn't," Daddy said.

"No," Momma said. "Not if I'm doing all the work."

"What are you two talking about?" I asked. "Why aren't you calling Mr. Creston back right this minute?"

I was so impatient, I bounced up and down in my chair.

"I'm thinking," Momma said. "I'm thinking maybe I should just do this by myself. Sell the sweaters on my own."

My mouth dropped open. It was a good thing I hadn't put another bite of beef stew in my mouth since Mr. Creston called.

"But—but—you said you couldn't do that. You said you couldn't afford to get burned again," I said.

"It is risky," Momma said. "But I'm not scared anymore."

I looked from Momma to Daddy.

"Why not?" I said.

"Because my daughter believes in me," Momma said.

# Chapter Twelve

On Friday, I wore the plain sweater with the heart on the front. No name.

Mrs. Burton gave me her biggest smile ever when I walked up the aisle to my seat.

"What's wrong, Janie?" Josh Hodgkins taunted. "Did you run out of names?"

"Maybe," I said. "Maybe not."

At recess, Kimberly and I played on the monkey bars together.

"I'll tell you a secret," I said, when we both sat on the very top, looking out over the whole playground.

"What?" Kimberly said eagerly.

"I don't even have a middle name."

Kimberly jerked back so far, she almost fell.

"Why not?" she asked when she got her balance back.

"When I was born," I said, "my parents said they looked at me and knew I had to be a Janie. It was the perfect name, they said. It was so perfect, they didn't want to put a not-so-perfect middle name next to it. They tried out every girl name in the ten thousand and one baby name book. And none of them was right. So they left the middle name line blank on every form they filled out."

I thought about how many times Momma and Daddy had told me that story. I could remember being three, four, five years old, cuddled up on the couch with Momma and Daddy. Momma's knitting needles were clicking away. The story had the same rhythm as her knitting.

"Wow," Kimberly said. "That's even better than having five hundred middle names."

"Yeah," I said. "It is."

I was so glad Kimberly understood. I'd never told that story to anyone back at Clyde. I'd been scared to. I'd been scared someone would think there was something wrong with me, just because I didn't have a middle name. But I knew Momma and Daddy loved me so much, they would have given me all ten thousand and one names if they thought I needed them. Just like they'd moved me to a new school when they thought I needed that.

That was why I'd worn the sweaters. I wanted everyone to see what Momma had done for me.

"I have a secret too," Kimberly said in a little voice.

"What?" I said.

Kimberly looked down at the ground, far below us.

"Remember how I said my best friend moved away?" she asked. "That was Larissa. I missed her so much! After she left, I didn't have any friends in Mrs. Burton's class because I'd always done everything with Larissa. And everybody else already had a best friend."

I hadn't thought about that bothering Kimberly, too. Kimberly was still talking.

"But then you moved in. And I thought, *She'll be my friend. She has to!* But you were good at math. You could do flips on the monkey bars. You were prettier than me. I thought, *I'll make her like me. I'll give her a coat. She looks cold.* So I gave you a coat. A new coat. I made my mom go out and buy a new coat because I said the new girl was really poor. But then you hated me!"

The coat Kimberly had given me was new? I blinked in surprise. I thought two things at once: *At least now I know no one will ever recognize it,* and, *How dare she!*

Kimberly had tears in her eyes. I couldn't stay mad.

"I was wrong, wasn't I?" she asked. "You're not poor at all, are you?"

Kimberly took a great gulp of air, then she looked like she was holding her breath, waiting for an answer.

I thought about how Momma and Daddy never had much money. I thought about how we were going to have even less money than ever now because Momma was going to run her sweater business on her own. And then I thought about how Daddy had said some things mattered more than money. I knew what they were now. And I had them all.

"No," I said, slowly. "I'm not poor. But I

was cold. I needed a coat." I swallowed hard. "And a friend."

A smile broke out on Kimberly's face. I think it matched the one I was wearing.

"I can teach you how to do flips, you know," I said.

We took off our coats so we could turn faster. By the end of recess, Kimberly could go backward and forward and dangle upside down. And she'd taught me how to do cartwheels out on the open grass of the playground. It was hard only because we kept falling over in the grass, giggling. We were having so much fun that other kids came over and asked, "Can we play too?"

But when the bell rang, it was Kimberly who scrambled up beside me. We both brushed the grass off and picked up our coats. And then, together, we ran back into Satterthwaite School.

Where I belonged.

With more than half a million copies of her books in print, **Margaret Peterson Haddix** has become one of the new superstars of children's literature. Her memorable and award-winning novels include *Turnabout, Just Ella,* and *Running Out of Time. The Girl with 500 Middle Names* is her first work for younger children. A former newspaper reporter, Margaret Peterson Haddix lives with her family in Columbus, Ohio.

**Janet Hamlin** has illustrated several fiction and nonfiction books for young readers. She lives in Brooklyn, New York.